Hysteria

National Bestselling Author

Myunique C. Green

ISBN 978-1-312-36412-7

Unleashing the madness building inside of my head.

Other Books
Available in Digital & Paperback

Fantasy
Everything That Glitters
Dead to Rights
Kingdom of Shade

Literature & Fiction
Psinder
Hysteria
Chaos
Observe and Report
Professional Development

Women's Literature
The C is for Complex
To Mend a Broken Heart
Sweet Savage

Mystery-Thriller and Suspense
Chopped & Skrewed
Last Seen
Compulsive

Short Stories
713
281
Minutes 2 Madness

For a complete list of titles visit: **MyuniqueGreen.com**

Where the Heart Is

Warmth courses through my body as I sit here; my face resting inside both palms.

"Another one," I order one of the men behind the counter.

He glares at me with obvious concern. "I think you've had enough, John."

Leaping up from the stool, a violent wave crashes over me and I lose my balance but somehow managing to support myself on the bar top. "You don't tell me..." my voice trails off with heavy slurs.

What sort of man have I allowed myself to become? This isn't me.

The bartender hurries around the counter to catch me as I threaten to fall to the hard tile floors.

"You do this every time. I'm not gonna serve you if you keep this up," he reprimands.

"Don't you judge me," I murmur, holding on to his sports jacket.

With his hand around my shoulder he tries to steady me, and for a moment I almost drag us both down until he lets me go. My body thumps loudly on the unforgiving floors.

"Get up, you fool," he demands, pulling on one of my arms.

I sit in a daze for a while, not wanting to move as the room spins around me. I faintly here the music in the background as my wife's favorite song plays. The tune still makes me smile.

Light smacks on my cheek pull me back into reality and the bartender helps me to my feet once again. "Who would have known!" I yell, laughing hysterically to myself.

He looks at me with an eyebrow raised. "What are you talking about? Known what?"

Shoving him away from me, I wobble towards the doors as if the ground were shaking beneath me. "I'll see you tomorrow!" I call behind me.

The cab is waiting as I approach the parking lot and the bartender walks quietly behind me, making sure I don't make an attempt at my own vehicle. He opens the cab doors for me and shoves me in.

"Behave yourself," he says, before handing my address to the driver.

The phone buzzes in my pocket as I slide into the backseat and I roll my eyes before answering it. "Yes, sweetheart?"

Lisa cries on the other end. "John, where are you?"

I pull the phone away and stare at the overly bright screen. "I'm sorry, baby, I'm on my way home now."

"I've been calling you all night! You were supposed to meet me here by seven o'clock. You promised me..."

Dropping the phone, I let her bicker with the leather seat.

"John! John!"

I run my fingers through my hair and pick up the phone again. "Yes, Lisa?"

"Are you even listening to me?"

As if she could see me, I nod. "Yes, Lisa. We'll talk about it when I get home. I'm sorry, I really am this time."

She sighs, and the line goes dead.

"She can be such a little bitch sometimes," I say to the driver. "That's why I prefer Mary. She knows how to make everything better. Eases the pain of being married to that woman, I tell ya."

The driver looks up through the rearview. "I know what you mean. Wives, huh?"

"I leave every day at six in the morning. I buy Lisa anything she wants, and she still finds things to complain about. She's ungrateful, is what she is," I chuckle.

Stretching across the backseat, I close my eyes and listen to the sound of the road as my head continuously swims. Mary is so good to me.

She makes me believe in me in me again. Takes away the empty feeling I harbor in my heart and the resentment I have for my wife.

I jolt up from the seat and peer between the clear partition. "Change of route," I say, reaching into my pocket and pulling out a business card. "I need Mary."

He reluctantly takes the card from my fingers and glances down at the address. "I don't think your wife would be too happy about this," he responds, sitting the card down.

Spit sprays the glass. "I don't care about that beast, she's holding me back. But *Mary*, Mary sets me free!"

"How long have you been married, man?"

I sit back in the seat. "It'll be 10 years next month."

He whistles as he exhales. "That's a long time to be married to someone you don't care about."

"It wasn't always bad between us," I whisper, struggling to remember the good times.

With his distractions, he pulls up into my driveway and blows the horn. When I look up at the two-story home I'm stricken with the urge to vomit.

She did this to me.

Lisa comes prancing out of the house, her hair in rollers and her nightgown blowing freely in the wind. I open the door before she approaches the car and throw up in her prized bushes.

"Oh John! Look at you, just look at you!"

I'm unsure whether it's judgment or concern in her voice and I slap her hand away as she tries to help me get out of the car. "Get away from me," I chide.

Tumbling out of the car, I lay on the ground for a moment, thwarting Lisa's attempts to lift me up. I hear the gravel crackle underneath the tires as the cab backs out of the driveway and for a moment, I wish it were me. For so long I've lived in misery.

I give in to her shrill cries and slowly get up from the concrete. "Pipe down, woman. I'm coming inside."

"I can't believe you, John. This is the fifth night this week! I thought you wanted to be sober? You were doing so well," she says, pushing me down on the couch and heading off into the kitchen.

As I peel my shoes off, I glare at some of her small trinkets sitting on the coffee table as they dance around in mockery of my vision. Lisa comes back into the room with an ice pack and places it on my forehead.

"I can't keep doing this, John," she whispers softly.

Holding the compress to my head, I lean back on the couch. "Let's just talk about this in the morning," I reply.

"No, you have to make a choice John. It's me or *Mary*."

Lifting myself from the chair, I catch her eyes. "Mary has nothing to do with any of this-- it's you. You're the problem!"

When she picks up one of the cups left out on the table, I briefly believe she's going to throw it at my head. "You talk about it like it's a woman for Christ's sake!" she yells, shattering the glass against the wood floors.

I look at her with disbelief. "You want me to choose? Fine! I choose Mary! I'll always choose Mary, you ungrateful whore! In fact, I'm gonna go see her right now."

Tears fill her eyes as she stares at me with disbelief. "You're a monster! A horrible, horrible monster!"

A sly smile smears across my face. "At least I don't look like one."

When she ran away, I got up from the couch and scoured the house in search of her car keys. Catching sight of them on the kitchen counter, I pick them up and drag towards the door. "Good luck on your own," I yell up the stairs before closing the front door behind me.

I speed down the dark road as if I'm racing towards my future. Tears burn down my cheeks as I grip the steering wheel so tight my knuckles whiten.

My sobs get lighter as I approach the bridge. "I only want to be with you. I've only *ever* wanted to be with you."

There's no explanation of why I treat her that way. She's a good, strong, and decent woman who's always seen the best in me. Although it shouldn't, the thought makes me frown. "She'll see. I'll *make* her see that I'm a better person with Mary. I can do *anything*," I grumble. My eyes can barely focus on the white lines as they sway along the road. Soon, though, my head begins to ache and the anger wears off. "What am I doing? I love my wife."

There's something about the sweet and smooth taste of tomato sauces mixed with the soothing vodka that make me stick so strongly to it. It reminds me of better days- days I don't want to end. But it also makes me angry- angry at Lisa for things beyond her control.

Afterall, it's not her fault she can't have any children. Chemo has taken everything from her since the day they first started injecting the poison into her veins. All we ever talked about were having at least two or three kids to fill our home with love. Maybe that's what started the division.

Pressing my foot further down on the accelerator, I jerk the wheel to turn around. Rain on the road makes it hard for the tires to catch traction and I lose control of the wheel.

"I choose you," I whisper as the car crashes against the steel rails and lunges over the edge, colliding with the cold water.

The Last Call

I sat down at my desk and stared out of the clear office glass.

It was such a beautiful day.

When someone tapped on the door I rolled my eyes and spun in the chair to look at the stranger step in through the door. "Can I help you?"

A solemn smile spread across his face as he pulled out a chair for himself and sat down in front of me. "About last night," he began.

I lifted my hand. "I don't want to talk about it."

When he pulled the chair closer to the desk, my pulse quickened, bringing along instant flashbacks.

"But I do, we have to talk about this some time or another. For God's sake, we work together," he said, placing a hand on the desk.

My eyes closed before I responded. "Please, Willie, just leave it alone. Let's pretend it never happened."

Last night had been a mistake; I never should have stayed as late as I did, let alone get that buzzed. Maybe it was all a set up from the beginning.

"How can you sit there and say something like that? Tell me the connection wasn't real."

A lone tear burned down my cheek. "I love my husband," I whispered.

In a flash, he was up from the chair, closing the blinds to the glass windows and shutting the door. I jumped up from the chair and stared at him as though he were mad.

"What are you doing?"

He walked towards me now, arms extended as if inviting me into his warm embrace. "Come here, please, let me hold you once more."

I stepped away from him as he stalked forward. "No, Willie. Just go," I begged.

My body gave into his arms and what little fight I had given was futile. He kissed my neck while his hands traveled down the length of my body.

"I told you," he whispered gently into my ear as the button was loosened on my jacket.

Another light tap on the door made me push him away and straighten my clothes. "Come in," I called.

Nineveh slowly twisted the knob and stepped in. "You have a meeting in ten minutes. I have the transcripts you wanted right here," she said, setting the papers on the desk.

I saw the heavy suspicion in her eyes as she stared between the both of us. "Thanks, Mr. Foster was just leaving."

She smiled. "Did you want to follow me over there?"

Willie looked at me from across the room and I straightened my coat once more. "Yeah, let's go."

I began to follow her out of the door, but Willie stopped me with a light tug on my elbow. "I need you," he said gently.

Blood rushed to my cheeks. "Ten o'clock."

With a satisfied smile, he closed my office door behind him and strutted down the hallway.

***

With the long leather overcoat tied tightly around my body I snuck out of the house in a hurry to get down to my car. Lawrence was knocked out across the couch while the television played on blind eyes.

This wasn't right.

I locked the door behind me and tiptoed across the driveway before I felt safe within the car. There was no denying the exhilarating rush of sneaking out; it reminded me of the times I used to go out as a teen.

The phone buzzed in my pocket and I jumped. "Hello?"

His voice was low and tempting. "Where are you?"

"I'm in the car and on my way," I replied.

It was as though I could feel the warmth of his body through the phone. "I can't wait to see you. I've been thinking about you all day."

After I back out of the driveway, I sped down the road in an anxious haste. "What about me have you been thinking about?"

He moaned. "I thought of your sweet smile and the feel of your smooth velvet legs as they wrapped around my waist."

A stolen smile swept across my face as I neglected attention to the road and as though they were the bright lights from heaven the entire car lit up.

My reaction was slow as I turned to see the oncoming headlights.

It all happened so fast. The bursting of the glass crashed violently against my face as my body rocked and I lay pressed helplessly against the steering wheel. The phone fell from my hand as I tried to remain aware.

The sound of the horn blared as I looked without seeing.

Whoever was driving jumped out and tried to pull me out, perhaps as calmly and as gently as they could. My ears rang.

I couldn't feel a thing as I sat there, probably in shock as red liquid filled by eyes. My breathing became difficult as an uncontrollable shake began to overtake my body.

Imprint

First, a rejection
An itch
There was joy behind the pitch:
"It's lucky!" said she
When it was thrown to me.

How worn, dull and greying!
Yet, a beauty that rests
Not upon the exterior, but within
The heart.

How cheap, weak, and failing!
Yet, what the eyes behold
The mind is blind to see
Such an invaluable expression
Of love.

It now sinks deeper
Deeper still
Like a heated rod
Pressed against uneasy
Flesh, until its brand is permanent.

However, not upon finger
Nor skin
Has it done the most carving
But o'er the muscle that beats
For her love.

The Party Foul

"I'm just saying, I don't think there is a man alive that can please you."

I look over at her with a half-smile. "You say that like it's a bad thing. If they think I can't be pleased, they'll never stop trying, right?"

Kas shrugs. "Or they'll stop and you'll miss out on yet another good man."

Car horns and sirens fill the silence as we walk along the busy city streets.

Grabbing her shoulders, I yell into her ear playfully. "It's all about the thrill of the hunt, baby!"

"Stop that," she says shrugging me off. "It should be about love."

Juice sprays the concrete in front of us as I laugh. "Love? That stuff is a disease, trust me, you don't want to catch it."

She walks awkwardly beside me staring down at the concrete. "Haven't you ever wondered what it would be like to be swept off your feet?"

Throwing her arms around me, she pulls me into an embrace and spins me around. "It's magical!"

I push her away and roll my eyes. "The only thing men are good for is sex and money. Some of them can't even have sex right, so mainly it's just about the money."

An all-black SUV slowly rounds the corner and parks across the street from us.

Sid.

Everyone knew he was bad news. Most of the guys around here worshipped him, but to me he was just my little brother.

Several people hop out of the vehicle before Sid steps out and they all wave.

Kas nudges my shoulder. "Aren't you going to say hey to your brother?"

I shake my head. "I don't have anything to say to him."

We all knew what he did around here, but no one did anything to stop it. If you even said his name too loud doors would slam and children would run in the house.

Must be nice to have that kind of power.

Only thing I've ever admired about him. The type of respect he commands. Yet I'm one of the few people who know that it all came with a cost.

Mama said he was possessed by a demon.

I snap from my thoughts and keep walking. "Are you coming over to my house tonight?"

"Yeah, come with me to pick up my stuff. This weekend is going to be the bomb, girl!"

I toss the can aside to join the rest of the liter on the streets and shove my hands into my pockets. "What if I told you I was nervous?"

She slightly bumps my shoulder then locks her arm with mine. "You? Nervous? You've got to be joking," she teases.

"I'm just sayin' that I don't know these people like that. I wanna be sure you're not walking me into some kind of trap."

Kas leans her head down on my shoulder. "Now, would I do that? What kind of best friend would I be?"

I laugh. "They kind that would bring Tiffany to my doorstep and watch her beat my ass!"

"That was one time! And I apologized," she answers, pushing me away. "Trust me, there are going to be so many cute guys at this party you're going to be on your knees worshipping me."

I trail behind her for a moment before she pauses.

"What's the matter?" she asks.

"Nothing," I answer, walking in front of her. "I just have an eerie feeling, that all."

***

Black leather sticks tightly to my body as I sit on my bed. "Are you almost ready?" I call out.

Kassidy stumbles out of the bathroom, releasing a cloud of steam behind her. "When are ya'll gonna get the air fixed in here?"

"Whenever you give us some money," I answer, getting up from the bed. "We're gonna be late, Kas. You're not even dressed yet."

She walks into the room wrapped in a towel and closes the door behind her. "No one likes to be the first one at a party anyways, you of all people should know that."

"So, tell me again how you met these people?"

Kassidy had the worst luck with ever getting anything right and I'd swear if her head wasn't attached to her neck it'd be long gone by now.

"Girl, you should have seen 'em. These two fine dudes just came up to me at the mall asking me if I wanted to come to their cousin's party. I said hell yeah!"

"Okay, but wasn't you with Vicky? Why she not goin'?" I ask curiously.

She checks herself out in the mirror and finally begins taking the rollers out of her hair. "Because you're my girl, plus, his friend was more your type anyways."

I smile. "What time will they be here to pick us up?"

Someone knocks loudly on the door and I stiffen as a new batch of butterflies start fluttering around in my stomach. I've never been this nervous about anything.

"That must be them, how do I look?"

My eyes start with the shoes and then work their way up her long caramel legs, wide hips and big hair. "You look alright. What about me?"

I spin as if on display and she gives me a thumbs up. Pulling my dress down a little more, we both walk out of the room and into the living room where my mother is passed out drunk. I gently shake my head before planting a red kiss on her forehead.

When I open the door, two guys, one tall and the other short stare with their mouths practically hanging open stare back at us.

Closing the door in their face, I turn to look at Kassidy and stare at her coldly for a moment. "Fine? I wasted a good outfit on these fools."

"I'm sorry they don't meet your high standards, Queen Sharese," she responds mockingly.

"Good night, Kas. Have fun."

I walk away. There was nothing wrong with them per say- if you're into short and round men.

Kas trails behind me, grabbing my arm. "Are you really gonna make me go by myself?"

Rolling my eyes, I glance back at the door. "You owe me," I sigh.

***

Muffled chatter and loud music bleed through the car as I glare out of the window at the large crowd scattered across the lawn.

I'd never been to this side of town.

Mama always told me there was nothing good over here and it was enough to keep me away.

I feel a cold hand touch my arm and I jump.

"Are you going to stay in the car all night, or are you going to get out and have some fun?"

My fingers fumble with the handle as I hesitate. Everyone here looked so much older than Kas and I, at least by five or six years.

Noticing my nervousness, Kas locks her arm with mine and whispers in my ear. "It's just a party, you've dragged me to a hundred of these things."

I nod and continue walking with her. "Stay with me, cause when I'm ready to leave I won't hesitate to go without you."

Nate come around and locks his fingers with mine. "This is going to be a night to remember," he smiles.

His touch repulses me more than his cologne and I stretch my fingers for him to let them go. Kas is already feeling the music and has left my side to join her surroundings with her date.

"Don't be like that," he says, running his rough index finger down my arm. "Let me go get you a drink."

I haven't finished my first drink good enough before Nate runs off to get me another one. I have no idea where Kassidy snuck off too and I could swear she did it on purpose.

She thinks I won't leave her.

"Come on, baby. Drink up, don't be shy," he says sliding the drink into my hand and rubbing my arm. "Loosen up."

I smile and raise the cup to my mouth.

Wait.

Something's fizzing.

Pretending to drink, I thank him for the refill. "Have you seen Kassidy?"

He shrugs. "I'm sure she's just off enjoying herself, like you should be."

"It's getting late, I should get her home, we have an early day tomorrow with Church and everything," I say pulling away from him and staring around the crowded room.

Nate yanks me back towards him, pressing his body against mine. "Tell you what, finish that drink and I'll take you home."

I look down into the cup again.

Taking a step forward, I pretend to trip, spilling the drink on myself and a few other people.

Nate leans over to pick me up, holding on to me tightly. "Are you alright?" he asks, prying the empty cup from my hands.

"I'm fine," I respond, taking a napkin someone has handed out to me.

"Can't hold your liquor, huh?"

I laugh to myself. Living in a house with a registered alcoholic, I'd learned how to keep down liquor at the age of nine.

The most devilish smile spreads across his face when he looks at me. He's obviously thinks his drug is already working on me.

Pulling away from him, I glance around the full house once again for my friend. I hadn't seen her since I'd gotten my first drink.

Nate pulls on me. "Dance with me," he whispers into my ear as though I wouldn't be able to tell that not only is he drunk but he also high out of his mind.

I smile. "Let me just go and use the bathroom."

Pushing my way past everyone, I let myself out and start to walk down the dark street. My heels clack loudly against the concrete and I curse myself for coming in the first place.

I glare down at the long road ahead. It hadn't registered before, but now I could clearly see that every house was empty.

I've gotten several houses down before a bright light shines behind me and I turn around to stare blindly into it. Maybe whoever it is will give me a ride out of here.

The car creeps slowly behind me, as though stalking. I turn around and start walking faster. They continue to follow me and soon I'm running.

All I hear is the sound of my heart thudding loudly in my ears and the roar of their engine. When I see a busy street ahead, I pick up the pace and suck as much air into my lungs as I can.

The car is inches from the back of my legs and I call out for help from anyone that can hear me.

Something cold and wet presses against my skin, waking me with a jolt.

"Good, you're awake."

A bright overhead light beams directly in my eyes and I try to sit up, but my body is in some sort of restraints.

"W-where am I?"

I try holding back tears.

A dark-haired man stares down at me with a mask over the lower half of his face. "You put up quite a fight, didn't you, young lady?"

Again, I try moving my hands, twisting and pulling, hoping the bands would give and set me free.

"Please, I just wanna go home, I won't tell anyone anything. Please, just let me go," I beg as tears burn down my cheeks.

"Well, this is your new home and frankly, tears won't help you here," he replies, wiping them from my face. "Now, let's get you all cleaned up."

"People are gonna look for me!" I yell, trying to yank away. "Wait until my brother finds out!"

He nods his head, and someone appears from the other side of the room with a syringe in one hand.

"That's enough from you."

I kick and scream as much as I can before a calming sleep falls over me.

***

My head is swimming when I wake up this time. The room I'm in is completely dark and it takes a moment for my eyes to adjust. I move my body slowly and discover I'm also free from the bondage.

"Hello?" I whisper, feeing around.

"Shhh… it's lights out," a soft voice responds. "You don't want to get in trouble."

"Where are we?"

I faintly see a shadow sit up. "Where you are shouldn't scare you half as much as where you could end up," she says.

"Why what happens…"

"Hey, go to sleep in there!" Someone yells into the room.

I lean back on the bed and let the tears fall. Why is this happening?

Our Last First Time

The wind twirled around in her soft curls as we sat outside on the porch that night looking across the yard and clear off into the future.

"Do you think things will ever change?" she asked, tucking her hair behind an ear.

I looked upon her angelic face, wanting to reach out and run a finger along its creamy ivory complexion. "Sure they will. We're going to be rich and makes lots of money one day. Then what can they say about us?"

She caught me staring.

"What are you looking at?" Redness flooded her cheeks and she looked away shyly.

"There's just something different about you tonight, that's all," I answered, returning my attention away from her although I found it hard.

When she got up from the chair, I wanted to pull her back down, make her stay here with me just a moment longer. Her company was all I had that was worth anything anymore.

And that was saying a lot.

We'd been friends for as long as I could remember but it wasn't until that night that I'd ever felt differently about her.

If only she saw herself as I saw her now, we could rule this world. *Together*.

"I'll see you later, Jacob," she said, stepping down from the porch and walking across the lawn.

I watched her for as long as I could as she sauntered across the street and into her house and though I wanted to wait a while longer, I got up from the seat and went in.

My mother had made meatloaf and everyone was gathered around the table. The room got quiet when I walked in.

"Is everything alright?"

I picked up a plate from the kitchen and walked to the table to sit down before replying. "Everything is fine, she just wanted to talk, that's all."

Pleased enough, she didn't ask any more questions just returned to being the mediator between my two older brothers.

They're always into it with each other. Arguing over which celebrity looked better in a bathing suit or which car went from 0 to 60 in less time. Sometimes I wondered if I was truly as weird as they said I was.

Not really in the mood for food, I played around with it for a moment, taking tiny bites until they wouldn't notice that I'd left the table.

"Hey, where are you going? You hardly touched your food," my mom called behind me.

"I'm full, mom. Got some studying to do for a test," I answered, continuing up the stairs.

As I laid on my bed I stared up at the ceiling wondering why I felt that way about my friend. It was all so strange and definitely something I'd never felt before.

Visions of her running around the golden straw fields behind her home played in slow motion while I imagined planting a soft kiss on those pink lips of hers.

My concentration was broken when a light tap on my window prompted me to get up from the bed and pull the curtains back.

There she was. Long blond hair pulled into a ponytail and wearing a white tank top with no bra underneath.

I tried to turn my attention away from them but I could see them a mile away, winking at me, wanting me to come closer.

"What are you doing?" I asked, pulling her through the window before closing it behind her.

"I couldn't sleep," she replied, flopping down on the bed.

I smiled when I sat next to her. We hadn't had a sleep over in a while, but only because our parents didn't think it was safe anymore. Despite our protest that we didn't see each other that way.

Well, I *used* to not see her that way.

She picked up a pillow and slammed it against my head. "Why are you smiling so hard, pervert?" she said with a smile.

I did the same to her. "You're the pervert."

There was a silent pause as we stared into each other's eyes. The tension was building to unbearable levels and I just wanted to lean over and kiss her soft lips.

"Would it be weird right now if I told you I wanted to kiss you?" she whispered.

My eyes opened wider. "I want to kiss you too."

She leaned in slowly, pursing her lips. I pulled her closer to me and pressed my lips against hers. For a second at first, then longer.

Then even longer.

Soon, our lips parted and our tongues danced around in each other mouths. I smiled.

"What?" she laughed.

"Did you have a cinnamon roll or something?"

She pulled away and covered her mouth. "I'm sorry, is it bad?"

I took her hand away and moved closer to her. "I like it," I whispered, joining our mouths once again.

***

My mother yelled from the bottom of the stairs, calling me down for breakfast.

Last night was the best night of my life and I couldn't help the all-out smile spread across my face. Something electric flowed through my veins as I got up from the bed and looked around the room for something to wear.

Justin barreled into the room. "I heard you in here last night, you little devil you!"

He pushed me back down on the bed and sat next to me. I smiled and shook my head. "I don't know what you're talking about."

The constant smirk on my face gave me away.

"Yes you do, was that Lynn in here last night?" He looked over on the bed. "How was it?"

"I think I love her, man," I replied.

His expression is overjoyed as Jace barged into the room next. "What's going on in here?"

Justin hoped up from the bed. "Jacob here got him some last night," he said, closing the door behind Jace.

I interjected. "Whoa, I didn't say all of that. We kissed, that's all."

Both of my brothers stared at me for a moment then burst out laughing.

"Do you really expect me to believe that after all the noise you made in here last night?" he pulls the cover back on my bed. "There's still blood on your sheets!"

I looked down at the bed and the red stain and immediately begin to panic. "Oh crap, what am I gonna do about this?"

Jace stripped the bed. "Wash your own sheets," he said, tossing them at my chest. "Do it soon before it sets in."

I balled the sheets up and looked for a place to stash them until I got out of school. A place my mom wouldn't find them.

But she *always* investigated things in my room.

"Jace, put these in your room until I can wash them myself," I panicked, tossing them to him.

He threw them back at me. "Ewe, stuff them under the bed or something."

Justin took them from me and tucked them under his arm. "I'll hide them. I'm honestly surprised at you, little brother. Welcome to manhood," he grinned.

***

When someone knocked I jumped up from my chair and bolted to the door. "See you later, mom!" I called behind me as I headed out.

Lynn stood quietly beside the door looking at me with that shy smile I loved so much. "Hey," she said, waiting for me to close the door to kiss me.

I took her hand as we walked across the grass and onto the street. "So, how did you sleep? You took off so fast last night."

"I'm sorry, I just got so confused. It was nothing you did. I enjoyed it," she answered while swinging our arms.

The wind blew golden leaves all around us as we walked along the concrete roads. There was a question on my mind, but I felt weird about asking it. I stopped and looked into her eyes. "What does this mean?"

She looked down nervously. "Well, I love you Jacob Miles."

We stood there on the side of the road glancing into each other's eyes for a moment before our lips connected again. But, I felt as though it was more than just our lips, but our souls.

Mr. Jenkins yells from his porch. "Hey, you kids better get to school before you're both late!"

I pulled away from her slowly. "He's right."

Her eyebrows furrowed a little bit. "Do you love me back?"

When I planted a gentle kiss on her check, her face softened. "Yes, I love you," I replied.

It was as though we both walked atop an endless sheen of sunshine as we made our way to school. Never could I have imagined that my life would change so drastically. So suddenly that my brain couldn't comprehend the thought of ever being without her.

All I remembered thinking that day was how everything was so perfect. Her bright smile a hope and promise of a better tomorrow.

Before we parted ways, I hugged her. "I'll see you after school," I said.

"Meet me by the field, no one should be there," she replied before disappearing into the crowd of students as she headed off towards her class.

"I'll be there," I whispered with a smile.

But, little did I know, that would be the last time I saw Lynn. Last time I felt her presence next to mine or the sweet ring of her voice as she told me goodbye.

Once You See It

I sit here on the bed
glancing out of the window and through
time, as stars fill
the night sky. Into a place
of happiness and inner peace. A time
when a hug could cure
everything.

It's this older life I'm afraid of.

For so long they've watched
Me grow, and blossom
into a woman
while they grow weaker
and wiser.

It's this older life I'm afraid of.

There are certain things
I've never prepared for, and
seeing her lie there
faced towards
the heavens, quietly napping
in eternal peace.

It's *their* older life I'm afraid of.

Love Never Fails

Rains beats hard against the window as I lay on the sofa staring mindlessly at the TV. Glaring down at my watch, I become restless and get up from the couch, pacing through the living room.

Nothing is working to calm my nerves. My hands still shake as I flick them in the air.

"Calm down," I whisper, continuing to move back and forth.

When the phone rings, I nearly jump over the whole coffee table to answer it.

He sounds as if he's out of breath. "It's done."

A smile spreads across my face as the tension begins to ease and my body relaxes. "I told you she would be easy," I respond, slowly sitting back down on the couch.

I hear a scream in the background and I wish I hadn't. It wasn't exactly like I condoned the work that he does.

Just admire it.

Plus, in moment like these it always seems to come in handy.

He clears his throat and though her screams are muffled now, I still faintly hear them in the background. "Do you have any more for me? What about the other one?"

As though he can see me, I shake my head. "That's all for now, I can handle him. I'll keep you posted."

The line is cut before I can say anything else and I sit the phone back down on the table.

There was one more problem I have to deal with. Philip is still wasting away in my attic.

A thump on the ceiling jolts my head upward. He'd better not be trying to escape again.

Rushing to the garage, I pull down the attic steps. Almost immediately, I'm hit in the face with a wooden chair.

I feel the warm blood began trickling down the side of my face as I try to regain my focus. Philip has already tumbled down the steps and now stands over me.

His foot lunges weakly into my side. "Surprise," he forces through clenched teeth.

I grin as I look up at him. His face is badly beaten and bruised, and the burns are so fresh I can still practically smell his skin melting.

When he leans down, I flinch, fearing he may hit me in the face. Instead, he grabs a handful of my hair and carries me back into the living room, making sure my head hit against the corners.

For a moment, I try fighting against him, but his grip is so tight I forced to comply. "What are you going to do?"

Drawers open and close as he bangs around the kitchen. He isn't saying much but as the silverware flies around in the counters, a paring knife slips his attention, landing right next to my hand.

Immediately I grab it in my hand, gripping it so tight I fear my fingers are going to pop off.

It digs into his leg.

The howl that blares from his mouth is nearly deafening as I scramble to my feet. He reaches out for me again, pulling on my dress; I feel its sharp edge dig into my back as he yanks me backward.

Pain cripples me.

I pull myself away from the knife, feeling sicker as it leaves my body. Air is getting hard to come by as I lose feeling in my legs and fall to the floor. Philip is still standing and looking down at me before stomping his foot down on my abdomen.

All I taste is blood as it spits from my mouth.

"See you in hell," he chides, while pulling the small knife from his calf and limping towards the door, giving me one final glance.

When I hear the door slam, I try lifting myself up from the ground—the counter helps me steady myself. Pressing my hand against my side, I momentarily slide in my puddle of blood.

Getting that out of the floor will be a headache. But for now, I have to at least live to see the cleanup.

My eyes search the house for my phone before I remember that I left it on the living room table. As fast as I possibly can, I shuffle to the living room, my head and body feeling increasingly weaker with every step.

I step on something left in the floor and I lose my footing, colliding with the ground.

It doesn't seem as if I'm going to be able to get up this time either. The table is so close, yet so far away as I reach my hand out towards it.

As dizziness sets in, I scrape my body against the carpet just close enough to pull the table towards me.

Successfully, I knock the phone down from the table and try to read the words on the screen. Pulling up the emergency menu, I dial out.

"What's your emergency?"

"H-h-help," I whisper grimly. My cry for assistance comes out more like a faint whisper and I've already lost too much to be concerned.

"Will it be Ambulance, Fire or Police, ma'am?"

I inhale tiny amounts of air as I try to respond. No words are making it out however; just raspy breathing and light sobs.

"Ma'am, are you still there?"

The phone slides between my fingers and I stare at it blankly as darkness begins to set in.

This is it. I think to myself.

I'm not sure, but I think I hear someone walk into the room. For all I know it could be the Grim Reaper coming to take me away from this land and into the next.

***

The air is sweet. So sugary coated it's bound to make my teeth hurt. I slowly open my eyes, surprised to find myself staring up into the clouds.

"Is this heaven?" I whisper with confusion.

Someone laughs next to me.

When I turn to stare into his face, I'm reminded of something I'd long since forgotten about. He stands there with a woman wrapped in his arms—smiles spread across both of their faces.

"Nah, this is hell," I answer, getting up from the ground.

For what seems like hours, my feet are planted in the same place. Fixed in the direction of the couple that was never meant to be. Placing both hands on my hip I clear my throat. "Excuse me!"

They glance over at me only to look back at each other seconds later.

It's Philip and Cayne—the backstabbers.

In confusion, I shake my head continuously. "No, no. Cayne, you're dead, or at least wishing you were right now."

They pay be no attention. Just stand there in a peace I once had. A peace that was stolen from me. I try pulling my legs up from the ground, but I can't seem to budge' the thought makes me panic.

Everything becomes white as an intense light forces me to shield my eyes as they both disappear.

My body son begins to ache, pulling me into reality. There's whispering in the room as I come around and I lay for a moment listening.

The steady beep of a monitor above my head lets me know I've made it to the hospital, and the fact that I'm able to barely open my eyes confirms I'm alive.

Or at least some strange form of it, anyways.

They whisper for a few more minutes, in a tone so hush I can barely hear them. "Who's there?" I say weakly.

My throat scratches as the words leave my mouth and my fingers wrap around my throat.

A woman in a white coat approaches the bed and smiles as she looks down at me. "How are you feeling?"

Pain shoots to my back as I try to situate myself on the bed. "I'm alive, so I guess that counts for something."

The doctor places a soft hand on top of mine. "What do you want first—the good news or bad?"

My stomach drops. "Let's start with the good news."

"Well, the good news is if you'd have gotten here a minute later we wouldn't have been able to save you. For the most part you're going to be fine."

I pull my hands from under hers. That much was obvious. The only part I couldn't seem to piece together was how I'd gotten here in the first place. Looking her in the eyes, I ask for the bad news.

Her eyes lower. "We weren't able to save the baby."

A tear falls silently down my cheek as I lay on the bed staring at the wall. "B-baby?"

I don't look over at her but the spike in her tone gives away her expression. "You didn't know?"

Wiping the tear away I try not to think about it. How can I be hurt over something I never knew existed until now?

Some things just are never meant to be.

The doctor changes the subject. "There are a pair of officers outside that would like to speak with you. Are you up for it?"

I nod. "Yeah go ahead and send them in."

Before she leaves, she checks some of the clear bags hoisted on poles behind me then leaves the room.

Two male Detectives step into the room and stand at the foot of the bed. The taller one talks first.

"How are you doing, Ms. Laurel?"

"About as good as I can be," I answer, still trying to sit up without hurting myself too bad.

"You've been out for several days, we've had people at these doors waiting for you to wake up."

A weak smile is all I can muster. "Thank you."

The shorter gentleman sits down in the chair conveniently next to the bed. "Sorry, I've been on my feet all day. You don't mind if I talk from here, do you?"

I shrug.

"How rude of me, we're Detectives Carter and French. Do you have any idea of how this happened to you?"

Images flash in my brain. First there was Cayne then Philip—and the crime they had to pay for.

One Philip wasn't through paying for.

But, I can't start there. No one must ever find out about that or I'd end up just like her.

In the end, all I can do is shake my head. "I don't remember much; it all happened so fast. Someone must have broken in."

Carter takes out a small notebook and jots down notes while nodding his head. "Did you get a good look at him?"

"No. All I remember is that his face was badly burned. I managed to stab him back. You should have found traces of his blood in the house," I answer.

They both look at each other then back to me. "That's the thing, Ms. Laurel, the house was wiped clean. The only blood we found was yours."

I frowned. "What do you mean? His blood should be everywhere, I stabbed him in the leg."

"Someone must have gotten there before we did.

"How is that possible? Wouldn't the police have arrived with the ambulance?"

"See, that's the thing. You weren't picked up by the ambulance. Someone dropped you off here at the hospital," French responds.

I slowly lift my hand to scratch me head. None of this is making sense.

"That's impossible, there was no one else. Are you sure? There must be something you missed!" The outburst torments my aching body.

Carter holds his hand in the air, telling me to calm down.

Detective French gets up from the chair, his old tired eyes staring down at me as though I'm helpless. "You've been through a lot. Take some time to think about it; if you remember anything feel free to let someone know. We're gonna keep patrol of your room, just in case whoever did this to you wants to finish the job."

They flash gentle smiles before walking out of the room and closing the door behind them. Its click makes me flinch.

At least it was nice of them to keep watching me. It still makes me wonder if there's something more serious I should be concerned about.

I lean my head back against the uncomfortable bed and stare up at the ceiling for a while. Had I'd lost so much that I can't even remember if anyone came into the room? Had Philip come in to finish me off but then had mercy on me?

Questions raced through my head as I stare at the blank wall trying to organize the thoughts as they come.

There's another light tap on the door and a nurse walks in with a bedside table in tow. "They told me you'd woken up, figured you'd like something eat."

I smile at her, but I can't think of eating right now. Not when there was just so much to think about.

She pulls the table closer to the bed before checking all of the monitors and placing a cold hand across my forehead. "How are you feeling?"

With so much going on at once, I'm unsure how I feel right now. About losing a baby I never knew I had, being practically dumped on the hospital lawn or being stabbed in the first place.

It was all like something out of a bad movie.

"How should I feel?"

Picking up the remote from the side of the bed, she turns the television on and sits the control back down on top of my leg. "Well, I hope you feel comfortable. You're awake and alive so you should be feeling grateful as well."

I roll my eyes. "I don't deserve to be."

She pretends as though she doesn't hear me then helps me sit up in the bed. "If you need anything, just hit that button right there and I'll be in to assist you. Try to get some rest, you've been through quite a bit."

"It would be better if I had some medicine to help with that," I say.

She takes the top off of the food then smiles at me. "I'll see what I can do."

When she walks out of the room my head leans back up against the bed. There is no way in hell I can let Philip get away with this.

With my eyes closed I hear the heavy footsteps of someone approaching the bed. I don't bother opening my eyes—nurses have been in and out of this room all day.

The abrupt stop they come to on the side of the bed makes me peer out a between the sliver of my lids. I only see the long dark overcoat and black gloves.

A spike in my heart rate as I begin to panic makes the monitor behind me go wild. My lids fly open, fully recognizing the man standing over me.

"W-w-what are you doing here?" I stutter.

How had he gotten past the officers outside?

He doesn't say anything at first just stares down at me with an evil grin. "You've gotten sloppy, Vivica. Although I must thank you for my latest gift."

The door handle rattles and he quickly slides into the bathroom, leaving the door open just a crack.

Nurse Ann comes into the room and examines me, then looks up at the machine. "Is everything alright?"

My heart is still racing as I look towards the bathroom door. Hopefully she'll follow my eyes. "Everything is fine, I was just having a bad dream," I answer.

She smiles then deactivates the heart monitor. "Well, the good thing about dreams is that they aren't real, right?"

It's hard for me to focus on anything besides the door as I respond. "Yeah, that's what they say."

Before she leaves, she asks me if I need anything then fluffs some of the pillows behind me. If I could, I would hold on to her hand and tell her about my uninvited guest.

As the door closes behind her, the man walks out of the bathroom and stands beside my bed. "Where is Philip?"

I look up into his stern green eyes and for a moment I feel like a child again. "I don't know. He got away after I stabbed him."

He shakes his head. "You never listen do you? Everything has to be your way; no use worrying about it now though."

The tips of my fingers go cold and travel up the length of my arm until I feel it spread over my whole body and soon my voice shakes as I talk. My hands tremble by my side. "What are you saying?"

Pulling something from behind his back, he jabs the needle into my arm mercilessly. "It's time for you to retire," he says.

Fear locks my body before his poison does and I'm not sure whether this is going to kill me or knock me out—it isn't long before I find out the answer.

Jackpot

Light rain sprinkles the ground as I glare out of the glass doors.

A loud clash against the tile floors snaps me back into reality.

"Hey, can you take the trash out?"

It wasn't really a question. No one ever really asks me if I want to do anything, they just expect them to get done.

The downside of still working for your parents at 25, I guess.

Nevertheless, I smile and pick up the large black bag. "Sure thing, Papa."

"When you come back in, I need your help in the back," he says, squeezing my shoulder.

He didn't care that I was just about to leave. Why should he? It's not like I have a family of my own to run home to.

Pulling the hood over my head, I step around him and head out of the backdoor.

A car horn blares.

I drop the bag on the ground and run around to the front of the building just in time to see a man dart across the street.

Mr. Harris yells for a moment before all goes silent and the sounds of passing traffic takes over.

Wiping rain water from my face, I stare across the street into the alley the man disappeared into. It looks like there's more than one.

"Syven?"

I jump. "Yes, Papa?"

"What are you doing? You're gonna get sick just standing out here like that."

Looking across the street again, I fight my curiosity and return inside the store with my father.

"What were you looking at, son?"

I shrug. "Don't really know, heard a loud horn and thought someone might need some help."

He offers me a seat. "Are you okay, son? You've been so distracted lately. Anything you want to talk to me about?"

Forcing a smile, I nod. "I'm fine, Papa. Just tired, haven't really been sleeping well."

Nightmares of being stuck here for the rest of my life plague me to no end.

Trapped. Like a hamster on a wheel.

"Why don't you take a couple of days off to get some rest? Uncle Joey will cover for you," he says, patting my knee.

***

I pound at my alarm until it finally shuts off and silence returns.

It doesn't help me get back to sleep.

Buster licks my face constantly until I sit up. "Good morning to you too," I say groggily.

Someone pounds on the door, prompting Buster to leap from the bed and run to bark at the door.

I look down at the clock. It's 7:45 in the morning and I haven't even gotten coffee yet.

"Cool it, man. I'm coming!" I yell, looking around the room for something to wear.

As though the window is open, a sharp chill blows through the room, ruffling my hair.

Ignoring it, I answer the door and Geoffrey steps into the room, nearly being knocked down by an overly excited St. Bernard.

"Good to see you too, boy," he coos.

I walk into the kitchen and start on a fresh pot of dark roast coffee.

"What bring you by, bro?"

He stops playing with Buster for a moment and stares at me for a moment. "Did you really forget?"

My eyes close as I think. "Nah but tell me what you're talking about so that I'll know we're on the right page."

Shaking his head, he leans on the bar. "Vivian's wedding is today."

"Right, right. I remember now. It isn't until this afternoon though, so why are you here so early?"

The smell of the coffee is almost enough to give me that pick-me-up and I think that's the moment when I realize how entirely too dependent on the stuff I really am.

At least it isn't alcohol.

"The suits are ready, figured we'd get a head start on this thing. Have you heard anything from Bianca?"

I load the toaster without answering.

"You didn't ask her, did you?"

"I was going to, but she has a boyfriend now," I reply as though it didn't affect me as much as it actually did.

She was my everything, or at least she had the potential to be. If only I could get more than a few words out whenever she's around. It's as if they run from me on purpose.

"Well, I don't know what you expected anyways. A beautiful girl like that never stays single for long."

"You should see the moron she's with though, a basket-case is what he is," I respond with a mouth full of bread.

"Good, means you might still have a chance. That is, if you grew a pair next time she's around. Now, hurry up with your breakfast, I gotta stop and pick up a new ticket before we get the suits."

I raise an eyebrow. "Ticket for what?"

"The lottery drawing is tonight. Jackpot is $250 million. I'm feeling lucky!"

I smile widely, but not for him. The thought of having that much money to myself sends a tingle up my back.

Bye-bye bakery and hello luxury.

After a brief fantasy, reality sets back in. "I don't why you still play that, you never win anything."

"Well, today's different, I can feel it," he says, pouring up a mug of coffee.

At the Men's Warehouse I'm buttoning the vest when Geoffrey pokes his head through the thin fitting room curtain.

"Ready yet?"

I turn to face him. "How do I look?"

He looks me over then steps in to straighten the bowtie. "Not half bad, come out here, let me see you in the light."

"How many people are out there?"

Grabbing my wrist, he pulls me out and stands me in front of the large mirrors.

"You clean up nice."

Her reflection stiffens me while mystic grey eyes look me over. So pure and gentle.

"Oh look, it's Bianca. What are you doing here?" Geo asks walking over to give her a hug.

I slowly turn. "Hey, Bianca."

"Don't act so shy, come over here and speak."

Why was I so nervous? My legs barely want to move as I step down from the small platform.

"I'm not being shy," I mumble.

"I haven't seen you in a while, Sye. How've you been?"

The awkwardness of the smile I show makes me blush. "I've been good. How're things with Kent?"

She smiles back. "We're not together anymore."

Geo clears his throat and nudges me with his elbow.

This should be my moment to ask.

My moment of boldness.

While the words are caught in my throat, someone calls for her attention.

"It was nice seeing you both," she playfully hits Geo on the chest, "and keep this one out of trouble."

How had he gotten so cool with her?

When she walks away, Geo slaps the back of my head. "What happened? She was practically begging you."

I shrug. "She'd never go out with a guy like me."

Glaring at my reflection in the mirror I flinch a little when Geo wraps one of his arms around my shoulder.

"Where's your confidence?" He asks, shaking me slightly.

"We can't all be like you," I mumble.

Pulling away from him, I return to the fitting room and pull off the suit.

***

Geo shuffles things around in the kitchen while I browse around for something decent to watch on TV.

"What do you have to eat in here, man?"

I look his way. "There are some leftover in the fridge."

Slamming the overhead cabinet, he comes back into the living room and picks up the phone. "Pizza it is."

Giving up on channel surfing, I toss the remote next to me and lean back against the pillows.

What's wrong with me?

I stare blankly at the screen, wondering how I'd ended up here. Renting a place from my parents, working in their store.

I'm supposed to be something by now.

Someone important.

Only seeing my parents on holidays.

"How'd you do it?" I say, nudging Geo in the rib.

"Do what?"

"Make people like you, get out of your parent's house, you know."

He thinks about it for a moment then shrugs. "I guess I never just waited around for other people to validate what makes me an awesome person. I drew confidence from that."

The lazy hamster I call a brain slowly starts spinning the wheels.

"Well, how..."

Putting his hand up, he silences me as the news intro plays.

Getting up from the couch I sluggishly walk towards the kitchen.

"Bring me a beer while you're in there!" he calls.

Before I throw a bag of popcorn into the microwave, the doorbell rings and I walk out to answer it.

"Get your own beer," I reply, tossing one of the coach pillows at his head.

As the numbers are called, we both stare blankly at the screen before I think it really sinks in to Geo that he's hit the lottery.

He stares between his ticket and the screen one more time before leaping up from the couch.

Buster barks with excitement, as if he could ever possibly feel the joy that coursed through Geo's veins right now.

"I can't believe it! Sye, pinch me, I have to be dreaming!"

With each jump on my couch, I feel my own heart becoming weighed down.

"Get down before you have to buy me a new couch," I say, tugging on his pants leg.

It wasn't that I wasn't happy for him. No one deserved it more.

Except me.

Why couldn't it have been me?

"I'll buy you 100 of these couches, buddy! I'm rich!" He yells, jumping down from the couch and running in circles around the living room.

"So what are you going to do now, rich man?" I ask with a wide smile on my face. "What's my cut?"

Although I was joking, he stops for a moment and stares at me. "Your cut? You didn't put in on this."

Frowning, I turn and walk into the kitchen. "I was just kidding, man. You can't take that thing in until Monday, what're you gonna do after that?"

His smile returns and he falls back onto the couch. "First, I'm gonna buy a boat!"

I laugh and sit next to him with two beers. "You can't even drive a car, why do you want a boat?"

"I can pay someone to sail it for me. I want to get a bunch of liquor and a bunch of bitches and set out on the open sea," he answers, clinking his bottle with mine.

"Sounds like the easiest waste of money," I laugh. "But definitely a boat trip I'd take any day of the week."

He pats my shoulder. "You don't have a choice, a Captain needs a First Mate. Besides, it's time you see the inside of a woman rather than a pastry."

I punch him in the shoulder. "We're not all whores in our spare time."

"I'm not a whore, there's just nothing that I love more than being between a pair of meaty caramel thighs."

Laying back on the couch, I try to hold the smile. He was the same now, but when it becomes real, money will be the thing to change him.

***

Today's Uncle Lou's birthday and the last thing I want to do is attend his party. So what if he's turning 98 years old.

It's pointless. He could die while he's blowing out the candles for all we knew.

Still, my mom has me working alongside her in the bakery whipping up eight dozen cupcakes like there's no tomorrow.

"So, Geo hit the lottery last night," I say while pulling a fresh pan out of the oven. "He's going to turn the ticket in Monday morning. It's close to 250 million."

"I'm so happy for him. No one deserves it more. Tell him not to spend it all in one place," she smiles.

Her words pierce me. She didn't think I was good enough either, as if I don't work my ass off day and night.

I take a deep breath. "He wants to buy a boat and sail the Pacific, I'm gonna see if I can talk some sense into him before then."

She acts unimpressed as she whips the crème filling, but I knew her, the whole neighborhood would know by the end of the hour.

"Well that's nice, but what's he gonna do to give back to the community?"

"I don't know, he didn't mention it," I reply, not realizing I've stopped in the middle of icing a cake.

"It's always important to remember where you come from," she says.

***

Fast taps on the door wake me up from a light nap and I slowly raise up to answer it.

"Come on, get up! Let's get out of here," Geo says, barging in through the door.

I rub my eyes. "Where are we going?"

He lifts a briefcase on top of the table and pops it open. "Check this out."

Gravitating towards the open silver case, my mouth gaps open as I stare at crisps stacks of hundred-dollar bills.

"Is this all of it?"

"Hell no, this is play money. So, put your clothes on and let's go play. I got a full day planned for us my friend."

There's another tap on the door and he swings it open for a tall, curvy blonde.

"Hey, baby, I thought I told you to wait outside, we'll be out there in a minute," he says softly.

Not paying much attention to them, I keep staring down into the briefcase. I should have this kind of money. Hot blondes should be waiting outside for me to pick up my charitable friend.

I shake my head and close the lid before turning around and heading into the bedroom. "So, what exactly do you have planned?"

"Firstly, I want to go to our old high school. Remember Ms. Krunkle? She told me I would never be anything, now look at me. A millionaire.

I gotta rub this shit in man!" he answers excitedly from the living room.

That was just like Geo, looking down on the little people. If it weren't for us growing up together I would be one of those people he looked down on, and deep inside I feel like he still does.

"You know she has cancer, right? I don't think she's gonna care very much."

"Even better, I'll rub it in by giving her the money to help with some of the medical costs. Even though she made me feel like shit my first semester."

It's warmed up just enough outside for me to feel comfortable in shorts and a t-shirt.

"I'm telling you man, this is gonna be a day to remember. Check this out," he says, tossing a pamphlet in my lap when I sit in the car.

"What's this?"

He points to the white boat on the front. "I just bought that, bro. It's waiting for us down at the marina. Gonna get some more women and alcohol and go down there and party all night."

The thought makes me smile, suffering through the intense jealousy that's started to build. Somehow I feel like I deserve this. It should be me instead.

***

Wind rips through my hair as I stand starboard. I never knew I enjoyed the smell of the salty sea until this moment.

Geo pats my shoulder and talks over the music. "You alright, man?" he spins me around, "There are party going on back here!"

I chuckle and snap away from my thoughts. He was right and there were a lot of women.

He pulls me away and into the arms of a redhead with more boobs than one guy can handle. My face sinks into them and she holds it there.

She smells good and reminds me of sunshine. Pleased, I wrap my hands around her petite body and sway back and forth to the music.

"That's what I'm talking about!" Geo yells above the music.

There's a nonstop flow of alcohol and I'm wasted before the sun sets on our party. Geo has disappeared under the deck and has been hidden under there for thirty minutes now.

"So, what's your name?" I slur, with my head in her lap and a bottle in my hand.

Her soft fingers trace across my face and comb through my hair sending a tingle up my back and straight to my second head.

He wants her.

"Tiffany, what about you?" she asks softly.

I nibble on her nipple when she leans over to set her drink down and it makes her giggle. "Syven, but you can just call me Sye," I answer, sitting up slowly.

Pulling her body close to mine, I fall back until she's on top of me. My tongue slides between her plump lips and waltzes with hers until Geo comes back up top.

I slide from under her. "Wait here."

Navigating through a dancing crowd of beauties and a few gentlemen, I find Geo. His hair is in disarray and his shirt mismatchly buttoned. Obviously, he'd just had a good time of his own.

"Hey, is it all clear down there?"

He smiles. "Found you something, eh? Go ahead, it's all yours."

Running back to Tiffany, I pick her up and sling her over my shoulder before walking to the back of the boat and down below.

She hugs my body tightly while her head rest on my chest. "So, how do you know Geoffrey?"

"We've been friends for as long as I can remember," I shrug.

"Must be nice to know a millionaire," she whispers, circling her index finger around one of my nipples.

"He'll always be the same guy that wet the bed until he was ten to me," I laugh, rubbing her back.

"So, what do you do?"

I roll my eyes. The one question I hate to answer; as if it could possibly matter to her anyways.

"I'm a pastry chef."

She sits up and looks at me wide eyed as though I'd just revealed some great and wondrous secret.

It makes me feel good.

"That has to be awesome. Designing beautiful cakes and cookies; the extravagance of it all. It's like art, right?"

If feels as though I'm looking at a glass sea when I peer into her green eyes. "Yeah, it's exactly like art. It allows me to express myself sometimes."

She smiles when she kisses my lips and pulls her body on top of mine, gently gliding me into her. "What else allows you express yourself?"

I smile and flip her over. "Let me show you."

***

"Here, take one of these," she says sliding a pill between my lips as we sit at the bar of a night club.

I'm not even sure what time it is anymore, and I wouldn't be surprised if it was a whole new day either.

Glancing out at the dance floor, I see Geo dancing in the middle of a crowd of women with glow sticks in his hands.

"You don't want to dance?"

I look at her confusedly as my heart begins to race faster and I feel like I must get some of the energy out of my system.

Jumping up from the bar stool, I grab her hand, pulling her onto the dance floor next to Geo.

He looks over at me with the widest smile on his face. "Are you having fun, brother?"

The fun is so real, it makes me wonder where I've been all my life. Had I'd really allowed myself to get stuck in the hamster wheel of the bakery that I've completely stopped living?

All of the built-up energy combined with the excess body heat makes me sweat and I start to unbutton my shirt, Geo has already beaten me to the punch.

"Yes, yes I am," I mumble, throwing my arms up in the air and letting the music move me.

***

My head is swimming when I wake up, and as I look around the blurry room, I don't remember how I got here.

"You okay, baby?" she sits up and looks at me with care in her eyes. Long red hair tumbling in large curls down past her smooth bronze skin.

"How did we get here?" I say groggily, laying back down and staring at the ceiling fan.

The sun shines brightly through the sheer curtains and kisses her skin as she rubs my bare chest.

"Geo dropped us off. You were pretty out of it last night. We all were."

I don't feel like moving, and if I could just lay here in her arms all day I would. Glancing over at the clock I see I only have an hour before I'm late.

Carried

Fly away with the dust

Spring away with the leaves

Leaves that turn to dust blow

through the sticky breeze.

Leaves and dust, dust and a leaf

Violent, yet peaceful

are remnants of things past, discarded

like the dust.

Who would have known that so much

Life depends upon a cycle of a leaf

And it's dust?

Hostage

An excerpt from
Minutes 2 Madness

My claws dig deep into the soft earth as I crunch fallen leaves beneath my paws. The moonlight shines through the trees touching everything with a sheen of silver light and fish jump around in the lake beside me as though they weren't afraid.

I lay down in the dirt along the water and glance out across the woods. Tonight is just like any other night.

I'm alone in the dark.

Only my thoughts keep me company. I have to admit that I love it though; at least it gets me away from the house and into the natural world.

Though distant, I hear footsteps shuffling around and I perk-up. A low growl rumbles in my throat to warn them that I'm here.

As they get closer, I smell their foul, musty odor and I sink deeper behind the brush.

A sharp cry sounds off in the dark. "Please, don't do this," a man sobs.

I peek up to watch Glen shift into human form. "Come on, Nick, man up," he responds, slapping the man senselessly in the face.

My heart beats loudly in my ears as I debate on whether or not I should do something. As self-proclaimed Queen of Stealth I can be out of here without them knowing.

Glen smacks the man to the ground and a low, yet obvious growl escapes.

Guess I'm in this, I think, lifting myself up.

"This has nothing to do with you, Naomi," he calls.

I don't leave, just stand here watching.

One of his partners lowers his body towards the ground and barks angrily.

"Get out of here before things get ugly," Glen warns.

Staring at the bleeding man, I see the fear in his eyes and it oozes from his pours.

"Get rid of her," Glen whispers.

The other dog lunges for me and I stand on my hind legs. His teeth bite down into my flesh before I dig into his haunches.

We roll round biting and scratching at each other, both of us trying to attain dominance. Once I'm on top, I place a large paw on his face and growl.

He struggles beneath me before I put him out of his misery.

Glens anger blazes as I kick up dirt on his friends face seconds before the Culpeo is replaced by a man. He looks between the both of us as though he's gonna do something about it. But he realizes that he's alone.

"You're gonna pay for that," he growls, changing back into a mutt.

I lower my body as he approaches me and we snarl at each other. He couldn't possibly be this stupid.

There's something of a dance that goes on before he backs away and lifts the man onto his back. I don't turn my back to him until he runs away howling.

The man hasn't said much and I wonder if he's still alive at this point. I rub my head against his face but flinch when one of his hands move.

He's hurt pretty bad but I still hear the faint beating of his heart.

Gently lifting him onto my back, I carry him out of the woods wondering what I should do with him from here.

***

The man has been asleep for the better part of the day, allowing me to have him cleaned and his wounds stitched properly.

I pace around the room in anxiousness, hoping he'll get up soon so he can get out of here. There's no telling what Glen is cooking up now.

Still, it felt good to actually have someone to care for and watch over. Call it the protector in me. Sighing, I drift towards the window and stare out across the on-going fields of green, watching the workers take care of it. Though being surrounded by people daily I always feel alone.

Always.

The man stirs behind me, faltering as he tries to sit up on the bed. "Where am I?" he asks groggily, holding the bandage on his head.

I have a seat in the bedside armchair. "You're in my home. Do you remember anything that happened to you last night?"

He strains. "Just bits and pieces."

"You want to tell me about it?"

When he looks at me it seems as though his face softens. "Are you a shrink?"

The thought of being such makes me laugh. "No. I'm just a concerned person."

He lowers his head. "Then, you wouldn't believe me if I told you."

I stand up from the chair and sit next to him on the bed. "Try me."

It takes a moment for him to get comfortable with me as I listen to the racing of his heart. He looks over at me with the innocence of a child as his emerald eyes search me.

"Were you the one that found me?"

"I had a paw in saving you, yes. What's your name?"

He smiles. "I thought that part was a dream. Thank you. I'm Nick."

I can't help but wonder why he's dancing around the real question, almost as if he was already trying to forget. Then, he opens up.

"Those guys, Glen and Gus, I owed them money. I told them I just needed a little bit more time but they weren't trying to hear it anymore."

When the doorbell rings, he looks around the room as if searching for a place to hide.

Placing a hand on his knee, I smile. "Don't worry, I didn't call them. In fact, Gus is dead."

The horror that overtakes his face almost insults me. It wasn't like I did it for fun.

"You shouldn't have done that!" he jumps up from the bed. "Now they'll be looking for both of us."

Of that I'm well aware. Still, I watch him dart across the room, picking up his shirt from the chair.

Harrison comes into the room. "Excuse me, Lady Valentine, a Mr. Colby is here to see you," he announces.

"Lead Mr. Colby to the conference room, I'll be down shortly," I answer, turning my attention back to Nick. "I have something to take care of, but please, stay here until I return."

He shakes his head. "I have to get out of here. I could be dead by the time you come back."

Placing a hand on his shoulder, I try to provide him a sense of comfort. "No one gets in here without a fight, okay?"

Leaving the room, I lock the door behind me then descend the stairs. When I pass Kayla, I toss her the key. "Make sure nothing happens to our guest upstairs."

The meeting is over just as quickly as it began and I make my way back up the stairs only to find Kayla asleep next to the door.

It wasn't induced.

Slightly searching her pockets, I take the key from her and leave her there before walking into the room. Nick is sitting on the bed staring at the wall mindlessly.

"See, nothing happened to you," I smile, breaking him from his trance.

He slowly turns to look at me. "Am I a prisoner here? Is that what this is?"

I look around the room. "Doesn't look like much of a cell to me. Don't know how many hostage takers serve breakfast in bed," I answer, pointing to the silver platter sitting next to the bed.

"If I'm not a prisoner, then I should just be able to leave," he bristles the hairs on my arms as he passes by. "Thank you for what you've done so far."

My back is to him as he leaves out of the room and as if they were waiting to hear him make a few more steps, I hear the howls outside in the yard.

I knew it was only a matter of time before they found my home.

He freezes in fear at the frame of the door and turns to look at me. "I'm not gonna make it out of here alive."

My shift wouldn't happen until nine o'clock tonight, which means I have a little over two hours left in this form for the day. "Come with me," I say, pulling him down the hallway.

"Where are we going?"

Patience has gradually grown thin with his cowardice. His thoughts are never clear and I don't have to be a mind reader to figure that much out.

"Will you just trust me?" I answer, before throwing him in another room. "Take your clothes off."

He looks at me oddly. "I don't know you like that."

Should I take offense? Do I look like a pervert, or even the type that would be interested in raping a man?

I feel my nails being replaced with long claws before I tear at his shirt, leaving four exposing shreds at his chest. "I said take them off. Dogs hunt by smell."

Looking down at his shirt, he moves so slow in take them off I wonder if he may have sustained some brain damage after all. So, I decide to help him, ripping everything at the seam.

"Now, put these on," I say, tossing him some clothes.

Kitty and Daniel burst through the door in a furious panic. This only makes Nick tense as he stares at the three of us.

"What do you want us to do?" Kitty asks, slightly out of breath. "They've gotten Simon, we have to go get him."

A pain hits my chest and it's almost as though a knife has been put in it. "No need, he's already dead," I respond softly.

Forged by Fire

An excerpt from Bloodlines:
Everything That Glitters

A light mist fell over the road as I rounded the curves in the highway. Traffic was minimal to none, so I drove slightly above the speed limit. Instead of riding with the air conditioning on, I wanted to feel the coolness of the mist and warmth of the outside air blow through my hair. Since I didn't have a convertible like Ash, I opened the sunroof, letting the breeze blow through my long hair.

I looked into the rearview, glancing at the road behind and catching a glimpse of my almond-shaped eyes. They were light hazel, in fact almost the same color as my wavy hair, which was actually closer to chestnut than hazel. I took one of my hands away from the steering wheel and ran my fingers through the tangled mess; I wished my hair was as tamable as Ash's.

Contrary to my loose waves, Ash's hair was straight and silky; its color was even different, almost the opposite. But I'd figured he'd just inherited the jet-black from Dad, while I'd gotten light-brown from Mom. Not what you'd expect from a pair of fraternal twins, but we were merely born on the same day because nothing about us seemed the same at all—except our last name.

Ash had let his pillow rest against the window, and he snored lightly. I let the window down on his side only. When the window had completely come down, the pillow flew out and Ash's head hit the frame of the door.

He bolted upright. "Are you freakin' serious?" He turned to look out of the window and watched his pillow fly momentarily, then slam onto the road like a brick.

"House rules still apply. No sleeping, loser." I repositioned myself in the seat; my back was beginning to feel strained.

"Well, while you were sleeping last night, I was up packing your shit out into the hauler. So sorry I'm not well rested, princess."

I shrugged. "You'll get no sympathy from me."

We were halfway through the longest stretch of highway in America before I had started to get tired and also before I realized the gas light had come on. "I think I may have passed up the last gas station a few miles back," I said.

"I'll look on the GPS and see how far up another one is to keep us from having to turn around." He picked up the monitor from the dashboard and typed in the search criteria.

I glanced over at the dimly lit screen and focused my eyes on the pinpoints. "I could have sworn we were closer than that when I last looked down at it."

He rubbed his eyes. "The next station is about two or three miles up."

"Yeah I saw that," I replied tiredly, glaring blankly at the road ahead.

"Oh, hey, I almost forgot . . ." He unbuckled his seatbelt and raised himself up to reach into the backseat. He pulled out two bottles of what seemed like grape soda from his duffle bag. "I found these on the counter in the kitchen when we first got back to the old house, along with this note . . ."

He pulled a note from his pocket and handed it to me.

I shoved it away. "You read it."

"Oh, sorry. Forgot you couldn't read," he teased, then held the paper up to his eyes. "In case you get thirsty."

"That seems random. We already have water. Mom made sure of that before she left this morning," I replied, ignoring his earlier comment.

"Yeah, it does seem a little strange." He held one bottle up into the fading sunlight and examined it.

I took my eyes off of the road for a quick second and looked at the bottle while he still held it in the air. The light-purple mixture nearly dazzled through the clear plastic, appealing to all five of my senses. I turned my attention back to the highway and motioned for Ash to hand me a bottle. "Must be a new kind of energy drink. Hand it over, I need it."

"How would you know that? There's no label of any kind." He examined the bottle, then turned his head to look at me and frowned as he tossed the bottle onto my lap. "Are you actually going to drink it?"

"I don't see why not. Seems ok to me." I twisted the cap off, took a tiny sip and swished the juice around in my mouth.

"What does it taste like?" Ash questioned.

I swallowed the last bit I held in my mouth. "It's actually pretty good and tastes like grape juice or something. Drink up." I then drank from the bottle until I had emptied it.

Ash looked at his bottle one more time, then shrugged. "What the heck." He took the cap off and consumed the juice.

Two miles later we approached the service station. A stabbing pain shot up my back, and I jerked the wheel of the car, causing Ash's head to lightly hit the window.

"That one was unintentional," I said before he could return the blow.

"You have a real problem, you know that?" he replied

I stared through the windshield as I eased the car off the road. "Take a look at this place."

The outside wood of the building was old and rotten, and there were more than a few shingles missing on the roof. I pulled up to the closest pump and put the car in park. "After this there's no more stopping, so if you have to pee you should do it now," I said.

"Yeah, right. You'd be lucky if I'm even still out here when you come out of there," he replied.

From the corner of my eye, I caught sight of a small rat bolt across the parking lot and into the woods. *I'm tough, I can do this.* I thought before stepping out of the car. I walked several feet to the entrance of the building and slowly pulled open the glass door to the tiny shack and walked in. Not a soul was in sight; the place was deserted.

I hate my life; I wish I could just run away and never look back.

I looked around the store expecting to see the person the voice belonged to, but I saw no one. "Is anyone here?" I called out. I fumbled around the moldy old store before I finally found something that resembled a checkout counter. Seconds later a small, freckled-faced girl popped from behind the wooden counter. Her dark-red hair was thin and matted, and her frail arms rested across her petite chest.

"Hello, can I help you?" she said. Her voice was raspy and dry, as if she hadn't had any water for days.

"I came to pay for the gas," I said and looked into my wallet. As I fished for my bankcard, I tried shaking off my unease with her appearance. She had cold blue eyes that pierced mine when I looked directly at her.

She reached her hand across the counter and smiled as if she didn't know she had creeped me out.

Of course, you do. What else would you come in here for? It certainly wouldn't be to see me.

I frowned and looked up. "You don't have to have such an attitude about it."

"What do you mean?" She looked confused for a minute, then smiled.

"Don't act like you don't know what I'm talking about," I retorted.

"Read my lips . . ." *and just calm down.*

I paid close attention to her cracked lips, yet after telling me to read them, they no longer moved. However, the words kept flowing.

You can hear me, can't you?

I nodded slowly. "But how?" I said, my voice beginning to crack.

The biggest smile spread across her face, and she came from around the tiny wooden counter to grab my hand. I got a sudden flash of the chills before shaking off her hands. "Forget the question, I'm clearly dreaming," I said.

I gave myself a quick pinch on the arm, then closed my eyes. I prayed that once I opened them this would all be just some silly dream and I'd actually be sleeping in the passenger seat of the car as my brother drove the rest of the way. Unfortunately, when I opened my eyes again I was still in the aging shack and the small girl still stood in front of me.

She placed her hands on her waist and looked down. *I know you don't understand now, but you will soon enough.*

"Could you just stay out of my head until I can gather my own thoughts?" I snapped.

She looked up and walked back to her station behind the wooden counter. "You drank the elixir. Now you have to deal with the consequences just like the rest of us."

I thought back to the drive there and the stuff in the bottles. "So the stuff we drank was some kind of super juice?"

"I guess you could call it that. It holds both a blessing and a malediction."

"A malediction?" I let the word trickle slowly into my over-active thoughts and wondered what could be worse than having to hear every thought ever processed by the human mind.

"No time for that now. Have you learned what else you can do?"

"How am I supposed to know? This whole thing is kind of new to me. Am I supposed to be able to do anything else?" I listened to the sound of my words; I couldn't believe I was actually buying this. Mind reading was a myth; it only existed in movies and comic books.

Taking in a deep breath, I tried to clear my thoughts again. But when sudden waves of visions and memories passed through my mind that weren't mine, I freaked.

"Stop it, stop it, stop it!" I yelled. Pushing my palms to the sides of my head, I tried to squeeze the visions away. I didn't deserve that torture.

Almost immediately Ash came running into the store. He grabbed ahold of my shoulders and turned me to face him. "Aliza, what's going on?" What happened?"

I allowed myself to slowly sink to my knees in front of a girl I'd never met before but suddenly knew like a best friend. "You have a lot of problems," I whispered.

"You don't know the half of it," she mumbled.

The visions were from hurt and despair in the girl's past. I'd managed to find her name through the mess of it all. "Corey, is it? While whoever has done this to me might have had pure intentions, I'd just like them to take this curse away now. I don't want it."

"If only it were that easy. I'm afraid you'll have to learn to deal with it."

I wobbled as I stood, looking at Corey and wanting to snap at her. I turned to Ash. "Did anything weird happen to you while you were outside?"

He shook his head and shrugged. "No."

I looked into his eyes, then shoved him away from me. "You're lying."

Before he could say a word, his thoughts replied for him. Panic, grief, and depression crashed over me. Visions of what had taken place whilst he stood outside fueling the car played randomly across my eyes. I saw his body split as his skin slowly began cracking, chipping and peeling like old paint- it was all like something I'd never seen before. A small headache began forming as I looked at the hazy recollection; he wasn't screaming, and he barely moved, yet his face was turned in complete agony. Tears flowed from my eyes as I imagined his pain.

Just as quickly as the vision had appeared, it was gone. I stood motionless for a few more minutes before breaking free. "Well, Corey, it was nice talking to you, but my brother and I are going to be leaving now."

I ignored the rest of the questions that had formed in my gut as I grabbed my bank card from the counter and held on to Ash's arm while I headed for the door. That store had officially become the Twilight Zone, and the faster I had it in my rearview mirror, the quicker I could pretend it never happened.

"Wait!" Corey pleaded aloud before thinking the rest of her sentence. *My father keeps me here because he knows that I have nowhere else to go. Please take me with you. We can help each other.*

"Absolutely not! I don't know you and I don't know your father, please, I just want to leave," I answered. As I got closer to the glass doors, my body froze on its own. I could only move my eyes as I tried glancing around.

Her voice was lower and firmer as she slowly walked in front of me and literally made me glance deep into her eyes. "Listen to what I have to say."

I moaned- even more waves of thoughts and hazy visions.

"You have to help me," he whispered.

Obviously thinking I'd just paused for fun, Ash brushed my arm and leaned to whisper in my ear. "We may need her."

The force that'd froze me allowed my motion again, yet I still stood still. "You don't even know where we're going or if I could be a serial killer, on the road with my sidekick to dump some bodies," I suggested.

After a pause she broke out into hysterical laughter. "That's funny."

I watched as Corey took a step away from her post at the counter. *Don't move*, she warned.

Standing frozen in place near the entrance of the store, I clung to Ash like a toddler scared to be left alone. When something started gurgling on the ceiling of the shack, Ash and I looked up, staring at the ceiling as it began to crawl with dark, transparent shadows. There were thousands of tiny screeches as the shadows traced across the top of the ceiling, singling me out and hovering over where I stood. Every bone in my body became agitated and angry as a dark blob inched closer to my face.

I let go of Ash and moved away from him, and the shadow followed me across the store. My pulse quickened as my blood began to simmer and boil inside, the heat-surge became so overpowering that my knees started to buckle beneath me, and I hit the hardwood floor. The ground beneath vibrated as I curled into the fetal position.

The burn of the fire only grew hotter as the shadow came closer. "Make it stop!" I screamed.

"This needs to happen. Let your body make the change," Corey replied.

"I don't know what you're talking about; I just want to go home!"

My body pulsated as the floor beneath me quaked and I found myself having trouble breathing. Ash never lifted a finger to help me as I gasped for tiny amounts of air. He just stood there looking down at me lying in front of the glass doors.

"If I die, I'll haunt you until you join me," I said as I slowly began to lose consciousness.

Mocking Jay

So many words

I never got to say

and the ones I did

don't take the pain away.

I sing for every time you called

and I didn't answer

I croon for every message you sent

and I greeted you with banter.

You were more to me than

can ever go into words, but

You're gone now

So I sing them for the birds.

Poor Decisions

An excerpt from 713

I should have known the moment I laid eyes on him that it was going to end badly. Everything about him was just too perfect: soft honey eyes with a gentle smile that warmed my heart to the point where I thought it'd ooze right out of my chest.

Vivica was away on business the day I came over to her house to drop off the papers and although I was just supposed to be dropping them off something made me stick around when Philip answered the door.

"I'm just going to leave these here," I said, hanging around awkwardly as he watched me from the couch.

It was hard not to look over there at his round eyes as I noticed him checking my body out. It wasn't the first time I've caught him doing such.

"Is that all you want?" he asked softly, almost as though he wanted it to be something more to linger around for.

As I looked around the living room I remember thinking of how the tension had begun to rise at incredible speeds. So, I shuffled around for a moment then headed towards the door without saying a word.

No matter how sexy he was, I wouldn't ruin the best relationship I've had with a friend in a long time.

In seconds he was up from the couch and standing in front of the door looking down on me with the smile of a thousand angels. "Why are you rushing off?"

I weakly tried to push him aside from the door. "Can you move, please? I have places to be."

His fingers brushed a loose strand of hair behind my ear and he leaned down to kiss me. Firm lips pressed against mine as strong hands traveled down my body to grab at my behind.

For a moment I was lost. It all felt so right like it was supposed to be this way. But, I snapped to my senses and pull away.

"This isn't right," I whispered. My mouth was saying one thing, but my body was singing a completely different song. It was telling me to strip him down to his birthday suit and make love to him right there on the couch.

Again, I tried to flee the scene.

"Look, I know you've been noticing me and well, I've been noticing you too. Don't worry, she'll never find out, she's gone until the weekend," his fingers play with the buttons on my pants, "you want me as bad as I want you."

Had it all been that obvious?

Well, temptation got the best of me and soon I found myself rolling around on Vivica's bed as the man she loved thrust himself deep inside me.

With every drive I felt a unique bond I'd never felt in this way with anyone before, and it makes me wonder is this the reason why she loved him so.

The sex was *incredible*.

We both ignored the sounds of a door opening as we focused on ourselves and the sexual desires we had pent up for one another. It wasn't until Vivica's face drowned in the complete definition of horror that we pulled away from each other as though we weren't guilty of anything wrong.

She didn't say anything at first just stood there looking between both of us.

No number of apologies can make her expression soften and it was almost like I could see the evil begin to grow inside of her at that moment.

"Both of you get out of my house," she finally said.

I tried apologizing again but she's trying to hear no part of it, just pointed at the door not even wanting look at me as I picked my clothes up from the floor.

Well, I had to admit to myself that it could have gone a lot worse, but it still didn't make me feel any better about anything. She wasn't supposed to be back for another three days.

Would it technically be her fault for showing up early?

Perhaps as calm as she could be, she didn't say another word to me as I slammed the door behind me and got into my car.

"What have I done?" I asked myself as I sat in the driveway. An even more important question should have been asking how could I make all of it right?

Philip hadn't come out of the house yet, perhaps thinking that somehow, he could smooth things over with her.

He must not know Vivica. At the most, she needed a couple of days to get her mind right so that she would even be able to talk to me again. That won't stop me from reaching out to her in the meantime though.

Though it may be hard to tell right now, our friendship meant too much to me.

Shattering glass and other things crashing against the walls of the house forced me to leave the driveway in a hurry.

An incoming call made me veer out of my lane a little bit and when I glanced down at the caller ID I was even more confused.

"Hello?"

Her voice was calm. "Come back, I think it's better if we talked this out in person, right now."

The line went dead, and I'm stuck looking between the road and the cell phone. It was no question that I was scared out of my mind. The key thing here was giving her the space she needed to calm down before we got into the heart of it all.

But, it was a mistake. She would understand that, right?

Luckily, I hadn't gotten too far away from her house and I was back in the driveway looking up at the house still wondering to myself what the hell I'm even doing back here.

The last thing I wanted to do was fight her. Don't let that confuse you with thinking that I won't, but only if I absolutely have too.

Vivica swung the door open once I was on the porch and a look half accented with a smile puzzled me.

"Come on in," she said.

Though hesitatingly, I moved into the house and jumped a little when the door slammed behind me.

"Look, before you say anything, I just want you to know that I'm really, really sorry. I don't know what came over me," I said, looking around the living room awkwardly for any sign of Philip.

I took the seat she offered and crossed my legs. Now, I just felt nasty. Unworthy to even call myself a woman. Real women wouldn't do what I did.

Especially since we considered each other sisters.

I wondered if she could see the struggle going on within me as I sat there on the couch staring across at the wall, waiting for her to say something that would start an argument and eventually lead to a fight on the front lawn.

It gets that serious sometimes.

"So, you want to tell me your side of what happened?"

I took a deep breath and started from the beginning.

"That's it, huh? You were just caught up in the moment?" she responded after several seconds of silence.

I shrugged. "Yeah, I guess I was. But, I'm a hundred times sorry, Viv, I just lost my head."

When she nodded it all felt unreal. The whole time I had been talking she just sat there listening to what I had to say, only stopping to ask one question. Overall, just letting me get it all out.

"I understand now."

There was something almost sadistic about the way she said it. Something that told me that not only would things never be the same, but inside her head she was thinking of a master plan.

Since I got here there has been no sign of Philip, not a peep, and since his car was still sitting outside when I left I'm wondering if he made it out safely.

"I'm going to need some time to let this all sink in, you know that, Cayne. I'll call you, don't call me," she called behind me as I got into my car.

Yeah, I knew it would take a while before I heard anything from her but at least we got this part out of the way without fighting about it. No ill words at all, even.

My mind can't seem to remain focused on one thing as I take the long journey back to my apartment on the other side of town, and the more thought I put into what happened the more I began to over analyze things.

Has she lost her mind or has two years of schooling finally paid off? Either way, I'm not sure what to think.

A phone call from Philip throws me in another loop and I thought twice before actually picking it up. What we did was wrong, and he probably just wanted to apologize for seducing me.

It was all his fault after all.

"What do you want?" I said, holding the steering wheel tightly with one hand.

He's whispering in short labored breaths. "Help me."

Cars flew by me on the freeway as I pulled over to the shoulder of the road and put the phone on speaker to amplify his sound.

"What's going on?"

There was a lot of banging in the background before the line went dead and all my attempts to redial the number only lead me to his voicemail.

"Unless you called to apologize, never call me again," I left on his phone.

When I got home I tossed my keys on the table and slowly started to peel my clothes off as I walked towards my room. Today was a long one and I just wanted to shower and at least try to get some rest.

The strange feeling, I felt in my chest did not seem to want to go away as I turned the shower on and let the steam fill the bathroom. I stared at myself in the mirror for a moment before finally stepping into the hot water.

It was a good feeling at first. At least it helped take my mind off of everything as I felt like I was washing it all away. But, when the feeling wore off I was left with just nakedness.

When the phone rang in the living room, I decided to go ahead and get out of the tub even though I wasn't going to answer it.

I had enough on my mind.

Water sprinkled on the floor as I walked out of the bathroom and into my room to search for something to slip over me.

I didn't know how I'd be able to sleep with all of the commotion going on in my head and now the phone was ringing every couple of minutes.

It better be important.

The number was unfamiliar to me, but if answering it would stop them from calling me back to back like that I was glad to do it.

"How can I help you?"

His voice was low as though he was growling. "Are you ready?"

I shook my head. "You have the wrong number," I said before hanging the phone up.

There wasn't much time to even sit the phone down before he called back.

"Are you ready?"

For a moment I sat on the other end of the phone waiting for him to say more. Thinking that maybe someone I knew was playing a joke or something.

"Listen, I don't feel like playing tonight. Find someone else," I replied, hanging the phone up a second time.

That didn't stop him from calling back and now I'm upset. "Stop calling my damn phone. You have the wrong number."

"Do I really, Cayne?"

I stared down at the number on the screen again. "Who is this?"

A low and slow chuckle rumbled through his throat. "Do I have your attention now, *Cayne*?"

The way he said my name sent chills down my spine and I couldn't help but sit down on the couch with a firm hold of the phone. "What do you want?"

"Are you ready?"

I took the bait. "Ready for what?"

He didn't respond.

"Ready for what?" I asked again, a little louder.

The line went dead and instead of calling back, I got up from the couch and went into the room.

A loud beat on the door stopped me in the middle of the hallway with a surprising jolt. As I turned to face the door my heart raced as if it would leap from my chest and tumble onto the floor.

My feet slid against the carpet as I moved towards the door. "Who is it?"

With the phone still in my hands, I locked in 9-1-1 just in case. A look through the peephole revealed that no one was out there yet I still wanted to open the door.

I didn't have to though when a card slid under the door, hitting my toe. There were no words that immediately grabbed my attention and it wasn't until I flipped it over that it drifted slowly back onto the ground.

Instantly I redialed the last number but wasn't surprised when no one answered it. I screamed at the voicemail. "Look, I don't know what kind of sick game you're playing but I'm not gonna be a part of it. Next time you call this number I'm going straight to the cops."

I hung up the phone and went into the room then threw myself over the bed. Vivica was probably just playing with me to entertain herself. Her sense of humor was twisted like that.

The question still remained on my brain that there was a possibility that this was a real threat. Sure, Vivica could sometimes be twisted but I didn't think she would ever do something to hurt me, let alone *kill* me.

Either way, I looked at the phone and sent her a text to give me a call whenever she could or wanted to. I'd still try to talk about it.

I straightened myself on the bed and crawled under the cover before turning the television on to let sound fill the house. Darkness and silence are two things that could never be mixed together in my book.

The phone rang once again but I ignored it, choosing instead to drift off into an unknown world of my dreams.

Perhaps they would provide me with solace. But with the day I had, I wouldn't be surprised if they, in turn, haunted me as well.

Fighting Chance

An excerpt from Last Seen

He walks into the office wearing an all-black Giorgio Armani suit with a solid red tie. All eyes are on him as he struts down the hallway as if it's his personal runway.

I swivel in my chair as I longingly stare out of my office door, trying my best not to look noticeably. His dark chocolate skin emits a smooth sheen when kissed by the sunlight beaming through the glass windows. My legs tighten together. The definition of tall, dark and handsome.

He's first stopped by Vincent who introduces him to Alice. I'm sure there was nothing that made her life more enjoyable than that moment. She tosses her hair playfully and shows off freshly whitened teeth with a fake, overly dramatic smile.

The longer I stare, nerves began building up again, ruining all of the progress I'd made since yesterday.

After Vincent dismisses himself, Alice takes it as her call of duty to escort him to my office. "This is the lady you're looking for," she smiles, ushering him further into the room. "She's going to take good care of you. Isn't that right, Kahra?"

Getting up from the desk, I return her fake smile and shake hands with Mr. Mack. "I sure will. How are you doing, Mr. Mack, my name is Kahra Daniels."

Alice looms around impolitely in the background. When I notice, I clear my throat. "I'm sure you have other business to attend to, right, Alice?" I narrow my eyes until she excuses herself.

After pulling an armchair for him, I walk around to my desk and take a seat. It was then that I began to look into his emerald green eyes. Puzzled, I pulled my chair closer to the desk than usual.

He caught on. "Yes, these are real and no, I won't rub my eye to prove it."

I chuckle and move paper around on my desk. "We aren't here to talk about your eyes, are we?"

His briefcase is opened moments later, and he pulls a stack of papers from it. "Entirely true. Firstly, I must inform you that my client is looking into several other publishers. Why should I recommend this one?"

"There will be plenty of time for you to decide that on your own. Our company speaks for itself. However, I will assist in informing you on the benefits of signing with us. There will be a presentation in the conference room tomorrow at three o'clock; this will highlight key points in the contract and who we are. I'm sure you are going to want to look over the contract yourself, so I took the liberty of printing it up for you so that I'll be able to answer any questions you may have."

He picks up the packet and briefly examines it before putting it into his briefcase. "Is this all you have for me?"

"What were you expecting?"

A broad smile spreads across his face, bringing his dimples out of hiding. "Would you like to have dinner with me tonight?"

Hours later the sound of smooth jazz keeps me from going insane inside a near-empty loft. I frantically look around the closet for something to wear.

Jenna startles me as she begins searching alongside me. "Is this a date-date or a business-date?"

I shrug. "Not sure, he didn't exactly say."

She pulls the one shoulder sleeve, little black dress I'd gotten from Ann Taylor down and holds it to my chest. "You can never go wrong with this, it's both business and party ready."

Taking it from her hands, I walk it out of the closet and lay it across the bed. "You're right. Should I be this nervous?"

"It's just dinner. Keep it business-casual," she answers.

I nod and inhale deeply. Casually glancing at the clock, my heart races when I realize how fast time has flown. "He'll be here in thirty minutes."

"Then you should not be standing around, should you?"

My hair is still dripping wet and I'm clothed in nothing but a robe. I rush to the bathroom to finish my hair and makeup.

Before long, the phone rings and I allow the doorman to send him up.

"I'll be finishing up one of the other manuscripts while you're away. Have fun, Kahra," Jenna says before leaving.

I can't remember the last time I've been on a date. Something about them seem awkward to me. Or maybe it's just me.

The dress is on and I've done the final touches of my makeup by the time he knocks on the door. Straightening my back, I open the door.

"Hello, Mr. Mack. Come in," I greet.

His eyes move up and down as he examines my body. After clearing his throat, he loosens his tie and says, "You look stunning."

With a shy smile, I close the door after he has entered the room. "Thank you."

He walks through the living room and over to the windows, glaring out at the Chicago cityscape. "You have a nice place; the view is amazing."

I nod. "One of the reasons I chose this place. So, I had my assistant make reservations at Alinea. If you've never been, you're going to love it."

"Good, I love trying new things," he replies while walking away from the window.

"Can I offer you something to drink? Wine, water?"

"No, I'm fine. I'll get something at the restaurant. Should we be leaving?"

Stepping into the other room, I grabbed my purse and keys from the dresser then head for the door.

At the restaurant, I stare across the table and smile. "About Mr. Farrell's manuscript..."

He shakes his head. "I didn't invite you to dinner so that we could talk about that. I'd like to know more about *you*."

Blood rushes to my cheeks. "Ask me anything," I grin. Relieved that this isn't about business.

"Where are you from?"

Momentarily holding my breath, I fought off another flashback. "I was born in Oklahoma, but I moved here when I was thirteen. What about you?"

He cracks his lobster before answering. "Originally from Texas, moved around a lot when I was a kid, finally found myself in New York and decided to call it home."

"What made you want to become a lawyer?"

"It's a long boring story," he answered.

I took his word for it. Somehow it was always a long and uninteresting story on how professionals became professionals. In my case, it was a typical scale of 'rags to riches.'

"So, tell me, what do you like to do for fun? Otherwise known as, what do you do when you're not working?"

I smile. "I'm always working. Much like yourself, Mr. Mack."

He gives me the grin that I'm sure has broken many hearts. "Please, just call me Brandon."

I barely have time to stick the key in the door before I'm thrown into a swirl of hot kisses. Slow moans vibrate my throat as my back presses against the door.

Reaching behind me, I twist the knob and pull us both into the apartment. His large hands grip me before sliding the dress over my head.

I fumble with the buttons on his shirt as he leaves a hot trail of kisses from my neck to my navel.

Putting the string between his teeth, he gently tugs my G-string off. When he comes back up, he lifts me, holding me tight against his hard body.

The keys fall from my hands and clash hard against the floor, leaving my fingers free to scratch at his wide back.

When my back smashes against a cold wall, a deep moan travels up my throat and out of my mouth.

Moonlight shines through the vertical blinds, illuminating his smooth chocolate skin. My legs clench around his body as he gently slides into me.

***

We've finally found ourselves in the bedroom after sex-stops all over the house.

The kitchen was the best.

I lay with one leg wrapped over his waist as we both stared each other in the eyes, smiles planted on our faces.

"That was fun," I whisper, clenching my leg a little tighter.

"I agree. Don't think that I offer all of my potential business partners this type of luxury," he responded.

"Potential?"

I turn him over on his back and climb on top. "What can I do to change that?"

His strong hands grip my hips. "Nothing you haven't already done."

Smiling, I lean down to kiss him. "I'll have the papers ready then."

He rolls me over. "Is that what this is all about? You think you can seduce me into a contract?"

I look into his eyes and grin. "That depends. Is it working?"

He grabs both of my legs and put them both up in the air. "You tell me."

***

It's our last day in New York. Jenna has already packed all of her stuff while I'm still struggling with my first bag.

"We should visit again, soon," I say to her while folding things into the suitcase.

She's moving to and fro in the room helping me pack things up, but she hasn't said a word to me.

I step in her path and stop her. "Are you ignoring me? What's your problem?"

Her eyes are tired and judging from the black rings around them, she hasn't had much sleep. "I don't know if I should tell you or not."

"Are you using again?" I assume.

She frowns. "No."

"Then what is it? You know you can tell me anything."

After folding a shirt and sitting it down, she takes a seat on the bed. "It's about Brandon."

I roll my eyes. "I'm fully aware of your jealousy."

"This has nothing to do with me, I just don't know how you're going to react."

"Spit it out."

She took a step closer to me and placed a soft hand on my exposed shoulder. "He's married," she whispers.

I pull away from her. "Don't lie to me."

Within seconds, she left the room, returning a moment later with her tablet in her hand. "See, its right here."

Glaring down at the screen, I briefly read the results of his background check. "Who authorized this?"

"They all submit to screenings. You just never looked this one over," she said before tossing the tablet on the bed.

I sat down on the bed, dropping a shirt I was holding. "We talked about doing so much together."

"How hurt could you possibly be, Kahra? You haven't known him for that long."

Hoping up from the bed, I angrily begin to throw things into the suitcase. "That asshole!"

"Look at it as a business venture," Jenna tries to console.

I look around. "Yet we're here! Sealing the damn deal ourselves. Mighty successful," I snap.

Storming out of the room, I hit up the minibar. My new best friend.

Jenna runs up and shuts the door, snatching the bottles out of my hands. "You're acting like *her*!"

I try shoving her aside, but she doesn't budge. "Get out of the way, Jen."

"No. Stop using this stuff as an outlet, you're better than this."

Taking a step back, I glare into her eyes and run my hand her cheek. "You're right, I need a new outlet."

I turn from her and head into the room, grabbing my phone and wallet before storming out of the door.

"Wait, where are you going?" Jenna down the hallway.

Refusing to answer and happy to see she wasn't going to follow me, I make my way down into the lobby and to the streets. Throwing my hands in the air to hail a cab.

"Wait for me," I tell the driver before getting out of the town car.

Two cars are in the driveway of the two-story home and colorful objects litter the front yard.

Toys. I think to myself. *They have kids.*

I don't know my exact reasons for coming here. Maybe I just want to see if this is true. If the Brandon I'd developed feelings for were an adulterer.

An eerie feeling crawls from my leg to my back and I do my best to shake it off. I walk carefully up the steps and onto the porch before ringing the doorbell.

Was I really being this bold?

My conscience begins to get the best of me and I turn to walk away. But before I can, the door swings open and a short, brown-eyed lady stares at me.

"Can I help you?"

"Is this the Mack residence?"

I hear heavy footsteps creak from behind her.

"What the hell are you doing here?"

Brandon pulls the woman away from the door. His face monster-like.

I am the one who should be angry.

"Honey, this is the lady I was telling you about."

Now, his wife looks equally as angry.

"I shouldn't have come here, I just wanted to see it for myself." My mind begs me to walk away but my legs won't move.

If his eyes were lasers, I'd have a peephole burned into my head where my face should be.

"Get out of here before we call the police," his wife practically growls. "And never bother us again."

I slowly back away from the door. I'd learned a long time ago that being confrontational never really got anyone anywhere. Besides, I was an adult.

"So, he told you about the all-night sex fest we had in Chicago?"

Ok, maybe not *that* much of an adult.

"He told me you seduced him, temptress."

I laugh hysterically then looked at Brandon. "Is that how it happened?"

His wife breaks away from him and picks up a nearby phone. "You have 3 seconds before we call the cops."

Dropping my smile, I slowly began backing away from the door. "As you wish," I say as though surrendering.

When they both back into the house, I look around the yard. Finding a loose yard-stone I pick it up and hurl it at the house. "Fuck the both of you!"

Two small children peak though the backyard fence. "And fuck your ugly ass children!" I yell.

Picking up one of their toys, I fling it at the fence. Forcing them to turn and run.

Seconds later, Brandon runs out of the house and tackles me to the concrete.

His wife trots out behind him. Only slightly trying to pull him off of me. "She's not worth it!"

There's a struggle as I try to kick him off of me. "Remember this position?"

The kids are back outside. Staring oddly at their father on top of another woman. Tears stain their faces, yet they never open their mouths.

Out of annoyance, I moan loudly. This certainly wouldn't be the first time I was jumped out and I never thought it'd be the last.

The wife kicks me.

I kiss her husband.

We roll around madly in the middle of the driveway. My breath is lost with every spin.

"You shouldn't have lied to me," I growl.

"Shut up."

Reaching around in the grass for anything I could get my hands on, I find another hard-plastic toy.

Bringing it forward and crashing it against his head, he rolls over long enough for me to get up from the ground and stomp him in the nuts.

I look down in favor as he curls into the fetal position.

I'd completely forgotten about the bitch until a toy truck collides into my back.

I fall forward, my entire body in short-lived pain. "You'll have to try harder than that," I mumble while getting up.

Forcefully fighting a flashback, I saunter towards her. A sly smile on my face.

I look over at her children. "You want to know the true meaning of pain?"

Their faces drown in fear. The older one steps forward and yells. "Leave them alone!"

After a single step, I lean forward, launching a fist with her name on it.

The cracking of cartilage in her nose brings me joy and a mild sense of satisfaction.

Her blood sprays on my shirt and she falls over on me.

Stepping back, I force her head to the concrete. "Don't start something you're not ready for."

When I hear distant sirens, I look around for the cab.

"That's right, bitch. They're coming for you."

I look down at her as she lies in a pool of crimson blood. "Shouldn't you be unconscious?"

My foot lands hard on her head. I squat down to watch her eyes roll back. "That's better."

Looking over at Brandon who's wobbling to stand, I wink. "She doesn't deserve you."

"What's wrong with you? You won't get away with this."

The blood trickling from his head compliments his face. "You should wear red more often."

Without another word, he sprints toward me, undoubtedly missing the rock I'd picked up. I aim for his head as he draws near.

Watching the object leave my hands and slam against his temple tenses my body.

He falls, tripping over his wife's body.

The children scream. I'd like to shut them up.

No time.

I jog over to the cab and look at the house. Neighbors have begun coming outside, running over to the couple and screaming kids.

Getting into the cab, I'm glad to find the driver sleeping.

I hadn't planned for this. I was provoked. At least that's what I'd tell anyone who'd ask. Jenna would understand.

My mind is in a state of unrest during the ride home. I should have been at the airport by now. This wasn't in the plans.

Glaring down at my hands, I try rubbing the blood away.

I should have taken the rental.

When the phone rings, I jump. My heart couldn't possibly beat any faster.

"Hello?"

"Kahra, where are you?"

"I'm on my way, I've had quite an interesting day. You may want to extend your hotel stay."

"Why? What did you do?"

Taking a deep breath, I try to calm my nerves. "It is highly possible I'll be going to jail tonight. In case that happens, you know what to do."

I hang the phone up.

When the car pulls in front of the hotel, I survey the area before getting out. People walk back and forth in front of the building. Shouldn't be entirely too hard to slip by.

I hand the driver a few bills then get out of the car. Immediately after I close the door they have me surrounded.

"Ms. Daniels?"

My eyes roll. "Yes?"

A strong-armed officer grabs one of my wrist and forces me to turn around with my head on the cab.

"You're under arrest for the assault of Mr. and Mrs. Mack."

He yells my rights over the blaring horns and chattering people.

The handcuffs are tight around both my wrists as he walks me over to his car.

I grin. "All this for me?"

C'est la vie

At daubed peace he lies here,
a man, proud and mighty with a bundle
of roses as withered
as the hands that cradle them.
An emerald reminder of a fate all too real.

Only his ears remember the shots
that fired off into the night.
And only these tired eyes beheld
the moon as he glanced up to notice
its light barely bleeding
through thick, black fog.

He raced forward, forsaking
everything worth anything.
>   *Today I will do what I want,*
>   *and tomorrow I will die.*
Never expecting to stop
or stand still and watch
as the smog cleared suddenly
and the world rapidly transformed.

A culmination of all,
time will remain
stagnant for none.
This is the way of life.

About Myunique

Myunique C. Green is a student, teacher, and author. The young writer independently published her first novel titled Bloodlines: Everything That Glitter against all odds in 2012. The book made it to the Top 10 of Amazon-Kindle's Bestseller/Top 100 list, and Myunique has continued to show her literature prowess with other titles such as Last Seen, The C is for Complex and Deceptive, as well as 713, a mystery crime tale that dominated the United States Bestselling Kindle Short-stories and remained a #1 seller for two consecutive weeks.

Honesty, Determination and Hard Work are her watchwords, and her works have been recognized by a few bodies, receiving a number of awards, including The Readers' Favorite Finalist Award for Excellence in Writing.

MyuniqueGreen.com

Instagram: @_cmajor_

Snapchat: @CeCe_Major

www.ingramcontent.com/pod-product-compliance
Lightning Source LLC
Chambersburg PA
CBHW022035170626
46808CB00003B/1206